Thank you to Sheila and Vance Ford for sharing their funny "Llama Tales" with me.
And to my daughter Ekko, who nursed quietly in one arm as I painted with the other. — DB

Edited by Robin Rivers
Proofread by Lesley Cameron
Cover and interior design by Elisa Gutiérrez
Author and llama photos by Lee Bonder

Printed and bound in Hong Kong

LIBRARY AND ARCHIVES CANADA CATALOGUING IN PUBLICATION

Bonder, Dianna, 1970-
     Eleven lazy llamas / Dianna Bonder, author & illustrator.

ISBN 1-55285-609-7

          1. Llamas--Juvenile fiction. I. Title.

PS8603.O53E44 2005   jC813'.6   C2004-906717-6

The publisher acknowledges the support of the Canada Council and the Cultural
Services Branch of the Government of British Columbia in making this publication
possible. We acknowledge the financial support of the Government of Canada through
the Book Publishing Industry Development Program for our publishing activities.

eleven lazy llamas

Dianna Bonder

WALRUS
B O O K S

D ale and Sheila owned a lively little farm, full of **chattering** chickens,

snorkelling *pigs*

and eleven **lazy** llamas.

Every morning as Dale fed the llamas,
he would call each one by name.

"Shadow!

Angel!

Eddie!

Star!

Lexie!

Rosie!

Rags!
Santana!
Mackenzie!
Kelsey!
Sara!

Time for breakfast!"
And every morning the llamas
would raise their heads, blink
their long llama lashes and go
right back to sleep.

One afternoon as the llamas napped, Dale stopped to check on them before he washed up for dinner. As he walked into the large llama pen, Sara, the smallest, perked up her ears then settled back into the warm grass with a polite **schnlork**. Dale chuckled and shook his head. "You are the laziest llamas I've ever seen. Don't you ever move?" He bent down, scratched Sara's velvety ears and headed towards the house.

That evening after Dale and Sheila had gone to bed, Shadow, Angel, Eddie, Star, Lexie, Rosie, Rags, Santana, Mackenzie, Kelsey and Sara opened their eyes, lifted their heads and jumped to their feet with one loud llama **thud!**

They snorted and pranced. They
hummed and they danced. They kicked
up their heels and flipped up their tails.

Schnlork, sneezed Shadow. **Schnlork**, sneezed the others. The llama party had begun.

*As the moon lit up the
farmyard, the llamas
danced beneath its golden
glow. Shadow and Angel
danced beside each other*

while Eddie danced
quietly by himself.

Star joyfully hopped
one way while Lexie
hopped the other way.

Rosie twirled around

and Rags bounced up and down, up and down.

Santana clapped her toes together

while Mackenzie, Kelsey and Sara skipped in tiny circles.

When the dancing stopped and the dust began to settle, Lexie noticed a small white blur racing around her feet. Carefully, she stepped backwards. Whoop! A chattering chicken flew out from under her feet.

Clack! Clack! Clack!

cried the chicken. Then spinning around, she hurried back towards the coop at the farthest corner of the farm.

Startled by the ruckus but curious to see where the
chicken had gone, Lexie hopped the fence and

followed the trail of feathers as they fluttered to the ground. One by one, the other llamas jumped the fence and followed her floppy llama tail through the darkness.

As the llamas gathered around the coop they noticed a bright light glowing inside. Sara, being the smallest, knelt down and carefully poked her head through the tiny doorway. As her eyes adjusted to the light, she noticed the chickens running around. They kicked up straw, scratched their feed and chattered loudly. Suddenly, Sara saw a small cluster of fluff poking through the gaps in the floorboards.

Chweep! Chweep! Chweep!

The cries echoed against the tin walls of the coop. The babies! thought Sara. The babies must have fallen through the floor!

Pulling her head out, Sara turned to the other llamas and pounded her feet on the ground. Immediately, Shadow, Angel, Eddie, Star, Lexie, Rosie, Rags, Santana, Mackenzie and Kelsey wiggled themselves into a perfect llama circle, listening as Sara described what she had seen.

As the moon sank into the early morning sky, the llamas gave one loud

schnlork!

and broke from their llama huddle. Sara led the others back to the coop and began digging at one end with her front feet. Santana followed Sara's lead, with the others close behind. Before long, all eleven llamas were kicking up dirt and flipping up rocks.

As the holes became deeper, Sara poked her head in to get a better look. But her head was too big and she quickly pulled it out.

Tired, she sat down, not noticing her tail had flopped into the freshly dug hole. Suddenly, Sara felt a small tug.

Jumping to her feet, she discovered a baby chick dangling from her floppy llama tail. **Chweep!** cried the chick.

Schnlork!

replied Sara. The other llamas watched in surprise, then quickly plunked their tails into each of the remaining holes.

Plonk!

Plonk!

Plonk!

Plonk!

One by one, Shadow, Angel, Eddie, Star, Lexie, Rosie, Rags, Santana, Mackenzie and Kelsey stood up with the baby chicks clinging to the tips of their tails.

Scurrying over and clucking with delight, the mother chickens gathered up their babies. Equally pleased with their rescue, the baby chicks nestled into their mothers' downy feathers, chweeping happily.

As the sun poked above the mountains, the llamas began to feel sleepy. Marching in a perfect llama line, they made their way back to their pen. They hopped the fence, settled into the dewy morning grass and fell fast asleep.

Dale and Sheila woke with the early call of the rooster and began their morning chores. When they filled the pig's trough they were greeted with a good morning snorkel. When they fed the chickens, they were welcomed with friendly chicken chatter. But when they entered the llama pen, they noticed the llamas were in the exact same spot as the day before.

Dale looked at Sheila and Sheila chuckled softly. "Those are the laziest llamas I've ever seen. Don't they ever move?"

Shadow, Angel, Eddie, Star, Lexie, Rosie, Rags,
Santana, Mackenzie, Kelsey and little Sara
just looked up, fluttered their long
llama lashes and fell right back
to sleep, dreaming of
adventures still
to come.